First published in the United States 1988 by
Dial Books for Young Readers
A Division of NAL Penguin Inc.
2 Park Avenue
New York, New York 10016

Published in Great Britain by Methuen Children's Books
Text copyright © 1988 by Mary Hoffman
Pictures copyright © 1988 by Joanna Burroughes
Printed in Italy
First Edition
OBE
1 3 5 7 9 10 8 6 4 2

Library of Congress Cataloging in Publication Data
Hoffman, Mary, 1945-   My grandma has black hair.
Summary: A child talks about her grandmother,
who is definitely not like the grannies in storybooks.
[1. Grandmothers—Fiction.] I. Burroughes, Joanna, ill.
II. Title.
PZ7.H67562My 1988   [E]   87-24654
ISBN 0-8037-0510-7

By
Mary Hoffman

Pictures by
Joanna Burroughes

My
Grandma
Has Black Hair

DIAL BOOKS FOR YOUNG READERS / New York

My grandma is not at all like the grannies in the books
I read. Storybook grannies have wispy white hair
tied up in a bun on the top of their heads.

My grandma has curly black hair
and she wears it loose.
One day I asked her if it was
really white and she got angry.

Grannies in stories sit knitting
in their rocking chairs.
My grandma can't knit for beans.

She made me a sweater once and it was too short—
with arms as long as a gorilla's.
My grandma usually sits on the floor.

Grandmothers are supposed to be wise and
dignified. My grandma is silly. Once she
got locked in the bathroom and instead
of shouting for help, she climbed out of
the window in her bath towel.

In stories grandmothers are
always wonderful cooks who
bake their own bread and cookies.

My grandma can't even make toast
without burning it.

Sometimes I wish my grandma was
more like the ones you get in fairy tales—
the kind of granny who wears a lacy
nightcap and looks very sweet and kind.

I don't think my grandma would
let herself be eaten by a wolf.

My grandma won't be called Grandma.
Or Granny. Or Nana. She says it makes
her feel old. So we call her Sylvia.

She is my mom's mom, but
my mom is much more sensible.
She says Sylvia is a little nutty.

Our school did a project on grannies.

We were supposed to bring pictures
of them when they were babies and
things they used to use, such as curling-tongs.

When I told my grandma, she said
I could take her hot rollers if I liked.

Sylvia doesn't really understand
about being a gran.

She should be quiet and comfortable,
with a pet cat for company.
Sylvia drives a noisy old car and
her only pet is a *very* rude parrot.

But there's one thing that grannies in books do that my grandma does too. She tells wonderful stories.

Not the usual kind, because
when she was a little girl
she lived with the circus.

My great-grandma and great-grandpa
were trapeze artists!

They live in Italy now, but my grandma has all great-grandma's sequined costumes in her wardrobe. She let me wear the pink one once.

When I tell Sylvia she's not like a
storybook grandmother, she just laughs.
She says, "Well, flower, *I'm* not going
to change, so the books'll have to."

My grandma lives with my grandpa—
but that's another story!